WHAT A DAY IT WAS AT SCHOOL!

Poems by Jack Prelutsky

Pictures by Doug Cushman

SCHOLASTIC INC.
New York Toronto London Auckland Sydney
Mexico City New Delhi Hong Kong Buenos Aires

MY BACKPACK WEIGHS A THOUSAND POUNDS

My backpack weighs a thousand pounds,
It's fatter than a cow!
I don't know how I carry it,
But do it anyhow.
It's filled with books and papers
That my teacher says I need—
She never lets me lighten it,
No matter how I plead.

Sometimes it tips me backward,
It's a wonder I don't fall.
Sometimes I have to stop and rest
And lean against a wall.
I tell you, from experience,
It's not a lot of fun
When you have to lug a backpack
That's about a half a ton.

I TRIED TO DO MY HOMEWORK

I tried to do my homework,
And I finished late last night.
It was our science project,
But I couldn't get it right.
I made a little creature
Out of seven kinds of slime,
Plus pudding and pastrami
And a lemon and a lime.

The thing began to wiggle
In a creepy sort of way—
I sensed that my experiment
Was going far astray.
It started making noises
That I didn't understand.
This was truly unexpected,
Not at all what I had planned.

It warbled, and it whistled,
And unleashed an awful roar,
Then bobbled up and down a bit
And oozed across the floor.
Then suddenly that thing I'd made
Went totally berserk—
My science homework ate my dog. . . .
I guess It needs more work.

WE'RE SHAKING MARACAS

We're shaking maracas
And beating on drums,
We're tapping on tables
With fingers and thumbs.
We jingle our bells,
And we play tambourines,
We rattle our bottles
Of buttons and beans.

We're blowing our whistles
And tooting kazoos,
We're clanging our cymbals
As loud as we choose.
We stomp up and down
On the floor with our feet. . . .
We love making music,
The sound is so sweet.

WE HAD A FIELD TRIP YESTERDAY

We had a field trip yesterday,
An annual event.
This year was really special,
We're all happy that we went.
We visited a factory
To watch candy being made,
And saw a million lollipops
On colorful parade.

We saw a vat of chocolate
That they'd warmed so it would melt,
And endless rows of gumdrops
On a great conveyer belt.
They gave us lots of samples,
And we giggled, roared, and squealed—
Our field trip was exciting,
Though we never saw a field.

I WISH I'D STUDIED HARRDER

I wish I'd studied harrder
For our spellink test today.
I'm sorrie that I didn't,
Now I'm feeling some dismaye.
I'd like to get a passing graid,
But don't beleeve I will—
I think I got *Whyoming* wrong,
And *Chyna,* and *Brazill.*

Though I don't want to make misteaks,
I make them awl the same.
It's no one else's fawlt but mine,
I have to take the blaime.
I tried to spell *Cunneddykit,*
But really, I just gessed . . .
If I had stoodied harder
Then I mite have passed this test.

A CLASSMATE NAMED TIM

A classmate named Tim
Is my partner in gym—
It's clear that I'm no
Competition for him.
We try shooting baskets,
He scores a whole lot,
While I hardly ever
Sink even one shot.

He's super at sit-ups,
And climbing a rope—
I'm useless at both,
And I haven't much hope.
But he never brags
That he's better in gym,
And so I enjoy
Being partners with Tim.

I MADE A NOISE THIS MORNING

I made a noise this morning
That I didn't mean to make.
It truly was an accident,
An error, a mistake.
I don't know how it happened,
But it suddenly was there,
Filled with great reverberations
That resounded in the air.

It made a strong impression
On the people in the room.
A lot of them reacted
Like they'd heard a sonic boom.
They looked at one another
As if asking, "Was it you?"
They were laughing, they were pointing—
I behaved the same way too.

I couldn't keep from joking
With the other girls and boys,
And never once admitted
It was I who made that noise.
Though I'm sorry that I made it,
From the bottom of my heart,
In a way, my brief eruption
Was a little work of art.

IT'S LIBRARY TIME

It's library time,
And I read to myself
A book about knights
That I found on a shelf.
I start to imagine,
The more that I read,
That *I* am a knight
On a powerful steed.

I conquer a dragon
To show I am brave,
Then vanquish a troll
In its dingy, dark cave.
I ride through the land
Doing deed after deed,
For we have a library
Where I can read.

IN THE CAFETERIA

I was feeling sort of silly,
So I took a bit of bread
And directed it precisely
At my buddy Benny's head.
"Who *did* that?" Benny shouted,
As he shot out of his seat,
Flinging carrots at Carlotta,
Who then threw her peas at Pete.

Pete took a small tomato wedge

And hurled it at Denise,

Who responded, catapulting

Macaroni at Felice.

Felice, whose aim is perfect,

Started pelting me with beans—

I believe that I am learning

What the food chain *really* means.

I KNOW HOW TO ADD

I know how to add, I subtract pretty well,
I multiply and I divide,
But I cannot seem to do fractions at all—
I've tried and I've tried and I've tried.
Will I ever solve twelve-elevenths times nine,
Or seventeen-sevenths times three?
These fractions are pains that my brain can't contain,
They're clearly a mystery to me.

Are forty-four fifths minus five and a third
As much as fifteen over two?
And how do I add six-sixteenths to a sixth?
I truly don't know what to do.
My teacher says fractions will soon become clear,
In fact, he does not have a doubt.
He's usually right, so I'll keep working hard,
And maybe I'll figure them out.

A MAN NAMED MISTER HOOBYBATCH

A man named Mister Hoobybatch
Is in our school today,
And we all get to listen
To the things he has to say.
He's giving recitations
From his stories in the gym.
He's written many children's books—
We've never heard of him.

He's big and round and jolly,
And he's lots and lots of fun.
He's telling silly anecdotes,
We laugh at every one.
In fact, we've not stopped laughing
From the moment he began—
We're glad he came to visit,
He's a very funny man.

I'M OFF TO
THE INFIRMARY

I'm off to the infirmary,
I've got to see the nurse.
I have a burning fever
And could not be feeling worse.
My head is splitting open,
There's a ringing in my ears,
My stomach won't stop aching,
I am practically in tears.

My nose has started bleeding,
And I'm getting dizzy too—
There is no doubt about it,
I have caught the Martian flu.
I'm breaking out in blotches,
And I've got an awful chill . . .
If I had done my homework,
I might not be quite so ill.

I'M LEARNING OUR HISTORY

I'm learning our history,
There's so much to know. . . .
A lot of it happened
A long time ago.
I learn how explorers
Arrived on our shore,
I learn of our leaders
In peace and in war.

I learn of inventors,
And scientists as well,
Of trips to the moon,
And the Liberty Bell.
There's one thing I'm learning
That makes me think, "Wow!"
We're all part of history—
It's happening now.

I DREW A YELLOW UNICORN

I drew a yellow unicorn,
Complete with polka dots,
A seven-legged elephant,
A pig with purple spots.
The sky was full of furry fish
All flying upside down.
An octopus was dressed in plaid,
A camel wore a crown.

I drew a green rhinoceros
That floated on the breeze,
Some bees as big as basketballs,
And blue spaghetti trees.
The penguins wore pajamas,
And a carrot flew a kite. . . .
My teacher says it's beautiful—
I think my teacher's right.

SHOW-AND-TELL

Benny brought a lizard
For show-and-tell today.
He didn't watch it closely,
And the lizard got away.
Carlotta stood and held a plant
That blossomed in a pot.
"I planted it myself," she said.
"I like my plant a lot."

Tim then showed some lightning bugs
He kept inside a jar.
Each one twinkled brightly,
Like a miniature star.
Felice showed off her hamsters,
Named Penelope and Spot.
"These are my hamsters," said Felice.
"I like them both a lot."

Amanda had a bird's nest
That she found beneath a tree.
Denise displayed her teddy bears,
I counted twenty-three.
Pete brought in some rope and tied
A complicated knot.
"It's fun to do," he told us.
"I like tying knots a lot."

I meant to bring my yo-yos,
But I guess that I forgot.
I spotted Benny's lizard
Perched atop Carlotta's pot.
I snatched it in a second,
Though I might have taken less—
Everyone applauded me,
I was a great success.

TEACHER'S PET

No one cares for teacher's pet,
It's really sort of sad.
He's always first to raise his hand,
Which makes some people mad.
They often call him awful names,
Like *Weasel*, *Rat*, and *Skunk*,
And moan when he gets answers right—
They'd love to see him flunk.

But teacher's pet is pretty smart,
So he is seldom wrong.
He also does his very best
To try and get along.
Everyone pokes fun at him,
And that's why I regret
That I am so unfortunate,
For *I* am teacher's pet.

I HAVE TO WRITE A POEM FOR CLASS

I have to write a poem for class

But don't think I'll succeed.

I know I don't know all the words

That I am going to need.

I cannot quite imagine

How my poem's supposed to be—

I've got a sinking feeling

I'm not good at poetry.

My poem must have a meter,

And it also has to rhyme.

It's due tomorrow morning . . .

How I wish I had more time!

I do not think that I can write

A poem the way I should—

But look . . . this is a poem right here,

And it is pretty good.

ISBN-13: 978-0-545-03624-5
ISBN-10: 0-545-03624-0

Text copyright © 2006 by Jack Prelutsky.
Illustrations copyright © 2006 by Doug Cushman.
All rights reserved.
Published by Scholastic Inc.,
557 Broadway, New York, NY 10012,
by arrangement with HarperCollins Publishers.
SCHOLASTIC and associated logos
are trademarks and/or registered
trademarks of Scholastic Inc.

12 11 10 9 8 7 6 5 4 3 2 1   7 8 9 10 11/0

Printed in the U.S.A.   40

This edition first printing,
September 2007

Acrylics were used to
prepare the full-color art.

The text type is Draftsman Casual.

For Alice and Clara
— J.P.

To Jack and Carolynn,
at last!
— D.C.

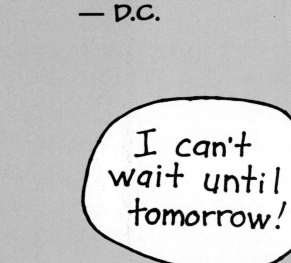